MW00886913

Sarina

BEVERLY FORGUS

ISBN 978-1-64191-029-3 (paperback)
ISBN 978-1-64191-030-9 (digital)

Copyright © 2018 by Beverly Forgus

All rights reserved. No part of this publication may be reproduced, distributed, or transmitted in any form or by any means, including photocopying, recording, or other electronic or mechanical methods without the prior written permission of the publisher. For permission requests, solicit the publisher via the address below.

Christian Faith Publishing, Inc.
832 Park Avenue
Meadville, PA 16335
www.christianfaithpublishing.com

Printed in the United States of America

CHAPTER

The Secret Place

I remember the day my mother died. It was late in the afternoon and we had been by her bedside the night before and all that day. She had not eaten for the past few days, so we knew what was going to happen, but somehow, we were still not prepared.

My mother's name was Leah and her strength was what held our family together. It was her ability to see our faults and love us anyway, that unconditional love that she possessed that made her a very special woman. I never thought she would ever leave us this soon. She was so full of life.

Even in her dying, she was faithful. She seemed to always have a smile on her face, and I know it was because she had such a special relationship with her Lord. As I watched her labored breathing slowing with each and every minute that passed, I thought about those special times we had shared together. I could talk to her about anything. She taught me so much about life and about God—all the caring, sharing, and the loving. He was the most important thing in her life and everyone knew it.

There was one special gift that God had given her. I called it the gift of "knowing." She knew God with an intimate and spiritual passion. She was always seeking a connection, and I know in my heart that she found it, for when you looked at her face, you saw a glow which was unmistakably the presence of God.

There was a special place she and I would go. It was our "secret place," my mother would call it. It was down by the river to the east of where we lived. The river Jordan was a narrow, twisting ribbon of water that came from the great sea in Galilee. It wandered through the valley searching for a place to find its own peace and rest. We would walk down to the first bend in the river where it widened just a little. The movement of the water seemed to have a calming effect. It was a place where you could forget all your troubles and just blend in with the surroundings. The water was so clear that you could see the fish swimming along the bottom. There were little rapids just above the place we would sit, and their babbling sound was soothing to the ears. There was a big tree that hung out over the water, its long slender leaves waiting to fall and drift along with the current. Near the tree, there was a large rock where she would sit, sometimes singing, sometimes painting, and sometimes she just sat there, engulfed by an inward conversation that only she and God could hear.

We were very close and this place was one reason why. I can remember our conversations just like it was yesterday. She taught me how to be true to myself and how to listen for God's encouragement when I needed it the most. I remember I once asked her if she thought I would ever get married. She looked at me and smiled and said that waiting for the right man to come along was all in God's timing. She said, "Just when you are ready to give up, it will happen." But she made it very clear that I should let God do the choosing.

CHAPTER 1

"How do I know for sure that someone I choose is the right one?" I asked.

"You will know," she said. "You will just know."

I remember leaving her bedroom for just a moment in search of fresh air. As I walked out into the afternoon sun, I could feel a gentle breeze on my face and a light fragrance drifted by from the vineyards, which reminded me that the next few weeks would be very busy and very sad. Our lives would dramatically change and that would be frightening. In my heart, I needed answers to some haunting questions, and somehow, I felt as though time was running out. I suspected that it would not be my mother providing those answers; however, knowing my mother like I did, I was sure she would leave me clues, ones that would help me find the solutions for myself. Funny, I was not even sure what the questions were.

When I came back to her bedroom, Leah was repeating two words that would be etched in my memory forever, "He's here, He's here." I asked her, "Who is here?" but she didn't hear me. She was in that other place where the only two people there were her and God, and they were so busy talking that she couldn't hear anything else. I felt the sting of tears on my face again—the same tears I felt each time I listened to my mother repeat those same words we had all been hearing for the past few days. I once heard someone describe tears as tiny messengers that carry with them a release of something from the heart.

Her final words were, "He's here. Find Him." For an instant, I thought she was getting better because her words were no longer broken, and though they were very softly spoken, they were directed and not scattered. Find who? And why? And then she was gone.

CHAPTER

Our First Encounter

After several months passed, I had learned how to stop crying every day. Mother's memories were so vivid to me. I took them with me wherever I went: into town, over to my aunt's with my sister, everywhere, except down to the river. For some reason, I wasn't ready to go there yet. Until that one particular day.

I think I was afraid to go before then because if I saw her there, even in my memories, I might lose her again. At night when I would sleep, I would hear her voice, and I wouldn't want to wake up. But that day, something in me was urging me to go back to the place where I felt the happiest. I needed my "happy" again.

Most of the journey was in the sun and the day was unusually warm, almost hot. But there was a breeze blowing through the trees, and it drew me nearer to the place where my mother and I would sit together and talk. She told me many stories about kings and battles, and arks and rainbows, and giants. It was as though they came right out of a storybook. Whether they were real or not real, the lessons they taught me about courage, faith, and obedience have stayed with me all these years. And if I am ever blessed with children, I will pass them along as my mother's contribution to their lives.

After about a two-hour journey, I could see the old tree leaning out over the water. I was sure I could see mother sitting there on that old rock as I had many times before. Her presence there was something I felt from deep within my heart, and the pain of losing her was still deep. I wanted to somehow go back to before everything happened. I wanted to remember every word she said to me and to stop the world so everything would stay the same as it was then.

Sitting under the old tree, I felt the moisture fall from the leaves onto my face, and as I looked into the swiftly flowing waters, I was blinded by the sun's reflection off the water. Deep in thoughts of the past, I couldn't take my eyes off the water, and I stared blankly into the brightness, remembering those special times, my eyes watering. Even as I heard the rustling of leaves behind me, I could not take my eyes from the river. Only when a hand touched my shoulder did I come back from wherever I was.

"I really don't want to interrupt your thoughts, but I also didn't want to scare you. Is your name Sarina?"

As I turned to see who was speaking to me, I saw the familiar face of a tall, dark-haired young man, about my age, I would guess, and I noticed he had a friend with him.

"Yes, it is," I said as I watched them sit down on the banks of the river. "Your face is familiar. Where have I seen you?"

"We did some work for your family a few months ago, building the wine house out in back of your house," said the young man. "I only remember seeing you once. We never had the chance to talk. I'm sure that's where you saw me."

I remembered now that it was just before mother's death. It seems that events of time are measured around that point of reference. I'm not sure that's such a good thing.

"I remember seeing you now," I said as I turned to the other one sitting closest to the river. "But I do not remember seeing you then. Were you there too?"

"No. I was working with my father then," said the other young man. "I don't remember being at your house before. Hi! My name is Jesus, and this is Stephen. It's nice to meet you, Sarina."

He was average in height with no striking features, but there was something about him I couldn't describe—almost like I had met him before, but knowing in my heart we had never set eyes on each other.

"Jesus and I have known each other for several years. Our families live in the same neighborhood in Nazareth," said Stephen.

We all smiled and surprisingly felt very at ease. It was as though we had all known each other for a very long time.

"So what brings you down to the river?" I asked, hoping to find out more about them. It was nice to talk to people my own age. I didn't have any really close friends. Most of my childhood friends were now married and had their own families.

"This just happens to be our day off," answered Jesus. "We have been working on a new house near Mount Tabor, and the time has come to rest and refresh ourselves. What better place to do that than here at the river?"

"It is beautiful, isn't it? There's a peace here that I can't seem to find at home," I said.

I paused for a second. My mother's presence seemed to overwhelm me with thoughts of her soothing voice and the fragrance of her spirit.

"Things are not the same since my mother . . ." Something stopped the words in my throat, and my eyes were blurring with those tiny "whatevers" again. I thought I could talk about her now, but the pain was still very real and very physical. I looked away, quickly thinking they may not see the pain in my face or the tears in my eyes.

"I'm really sorry about your mother," said Stephen as he tried to carry the conversation to a more positive direction. I could feel Jesus watching me closely, somehow seeing through to my heart, knowing I was carrying almost more than I could handle.

"She was well known and very well thought of in our town," said Stephen. "When my father and I were building the wine house, I would hear her singing. She had a beautiful voice."

I wanted to tell Stephen how I loved her voice too—that she was a beautiful lady—I wanted to tell them both that this world lost something beautiful when she died. I wanted to tell them how much it hurt inside now that she was gone. But I couldn't say anything. And I really didn't want to start a new friendship this way.

I took a deep breath and managed to murmur a thank you, or something to that affect. But then Jesus's eyes caught mine, and it was like he could see down into my very soul.

"God is always close to those whose hearts are breaking. He knows what a burden grief can be, and He will provide a way for you to get through it. Sometimes, He provides refuge and comfort in newfound friends."

Jesus had a gentle voice that was very soothing and he comforted me in a way I had never known before. The sound of his voice was like the rippling waters of the river, and it calmed me in a way that was almost indescribable.

"Jesus has this gift of always knowing the right things to say," said Stephen. He explained that they had been best friends since they were twelve years old, when they met each other in Jerusalem.

"We were there for the Passover that week, and the city was busy as usual," explained Stephen. "I was just playing around with some friends when I saw this old man with an old weather-beaten cart, talking to a young boy about our age. I decided to get closer so I could hear their conversation and found out that the man had been inside, looking for supplies when someone had stolen his donkey. This young boy saw that the old man was not strong enough to pull the cart himself, so he immediately lifted the tongue of the cart and began pulling the cart with the old man following behind. I thought he could use the help, so I ran over and helped him pull it to where the man was staying. And that is how Jesus and I first met."

"After talking for a while, we realized that we lived in the same village," said Jesus. "Stephen had just moved to Nazareth with his family. I guess you might say we've been best friends ever since."

"We spent the rest of the week together there in Jerusalem. When it came time to leave for home, Jesus was nowhere to be found. I thought he had already left with his parents. So I would just reconnect with him when we got home," said Stephen. "I didn't realize he stayed behind all by himself."

"My parents were not happy with me," said Jesus. "I was not trying to be disobedient. I guess I just got caught up in all the activities. They found me in the temple. There was so much to learn and the priests and teachers were asking and discussing such important questions."

"Your parents were worried about you, Jesus," said Stephen. "Jerusalem is not a safe place to be when you are twelve and alone. But when they got back, we saw each other almost every day. Joseph, that's Jesus's father, and my father taught us both how to build things and we've been doing things together ever since."

"I have never been to Jerusalem," I said. "Tell me more about the city and how they celebrate Passover."

As Jesus and Stephen began to share more experiences with me, I was beginning to feel normal again. Normal for me was when I would sing in the morning and smile at the wind when it would swirl the leaves into a circle that danced through the air. Their presence was making me feel free and new. They talked about their friendship and how good it was to have someone to talk to when things were hard to deal with. I felt a new hope being born, and just maybe these two new friends might be an important part of it.

After meeting Stephen and Jesus and spending most of the day down at the river, we all walked together back to the house. It was a day to remember. You might even call it a day of therapy for me.

CHAPTER

Meet the Family

At the foot of Mt. Tabor was a small village called Nain, my home. Within easy walking distance was Nazareth to the northwest and the river to the east.

The land was very fertile, and my father had a vineyard from which he made wine. He was well known in the area as being the one to call upon when quality was important.

My brother Jonathan was a needed help to him as the demand for his wine grew into almost more than he could manage. They had a very close relationship, Jonathan and my father, almost to the point of shutting everyone else out. I'm beginning to think that their relationship was all in God's plan, for Father would need someone to talk to when Mother would no longer be there for him.

My only sister, Rachel, was younger than I, and eyes have never seen nor have ears ever heard the level of exuberance she could display. A "bundle of pure joy" was what others said about her, and what they said was true. She could take any day and make it happy—just a gift she inherited from our mother.

She and mother traveled to Nazareth many times during the week to help my Aunt Shalee care for her eight children. My mother's sister was always strong and fully able to care for them herself until my uncle died about seven years ago. Since he had no other family of his own to care for her, my mother and Rachel began to sew for the other women there so that my aunt could support her family. So, as Jonathan helped my father, and Rachel and mother helped Aunt Shalee, I was left with the task of keeping our house in Nain.

The day had quickly turned into twilight as I said my goodbyes to Stephen and Jesus and started into the house. I knew Rachel was home, just like I knew the sun would shine the next morning. She was putting dinner on the table, and when I entered the house, I heard her telling Jonathan about one of Aunt Shalee's children, Haimon.

". . . and right there, in front of everybody, he kissed her! I couldn't believe it! It was so romantic. Aunt Shalee never saw a thing. He told me later that he would marry her tomorrow if that were possible. He said he doesn't think all that 'tradition,' as he puts it, is that important. Can you believe it?"

"So who's the lucky girl this week?" I added to let them know I was home. "He's always falling in love with someone and my guess is this won't be the last time."

"Oh, Sarina, you'll never believe it! She's someone he met only last week," said Rachel as she sat down at the table. "Her name is Tomar, Tomerrah, or something like that. You would think a man his age would be a little more selective about who he wants to marry. At least get to know more about her! I know he's my cousin, but he needs to grow up before he even thinks about a marriage."

Jonathan came alive when he heard his baby sister talk about growing up. "Look who's talking about growing up. How old are you now, twenty-one? And are you married? I say let

Haimon take his time while he can. The day will come when one of his girlfriends' fathers will say yes, and then he'll be matched for the rest of his life! And that's a very long time for someone his age!"

My brother was almost twenty-four, and he had not yet found anyone he wanted to have as a wife. Mother had even considered a matchmaker!

"So, do you think you'll ever find the perfect girl for you?" I asked, not really expecting the answer I received.

"She will have to be very spiritual, hardworking, obedient, beautiful inside and out, and she will have to love God and sing beautifully, just like . . . just like mother," he said.

Jonathan's voice dropped as he spoke softly about her. He didn't talk much about her death and neither did Father. So when this came out of his mouth, Rachel and I couldn't find anything else to say to him. And to render Rachel speechless in any situation was a miracle at best!

I'm not sure how long the three of us sat there, saying nothing, thinking everything, remembering and mourning once again. We only came back to the present when we heard Father come through the door.

Rachel was the first to speak. "It's about time, Father. How could you see out there in the dark? Your dinner is ready for you."

Father was not much of a conversationalist. He was a dear man who tolerated much from his family, but when it came to expressing his emotions, he fell short of average.

"Thanks. I'll wash up," he said. He looked tired and older every day. He worked too hard. I'm glad Jonathan was here to help him.

As he left the room, I reminded the others that we should keep the conversation directed away from mother's death. We should try bringing laughter and joy into our house once again.

"Mother would have wanted us to go on with life, to be strong in her absence. Let's try to do what I know she must have prayed for," I said.

For the remaining part of dinner, we were able to do just that. Father mentioned a long trip tomorrow to deliver wine to a family in Jericho. He asked Jonathan to help him load before sunrise in the morning so that they could get an early start. Without mentioning mother's name again, the evening was without tears, without sadness. Maybe someday we could talk about it and be joyful. I prayed for that day to come soon.

As Rachel cleaned up after dinner, I began to pick up things in the living room. With everything in place, Rachel and I went to bed. It had been a long day.

CHAPTER

The Wave, the Cloth, and the Children

As I lay there in my bed, I thought about Rachel and how she was handling our mother's death. At least she did talk about it. And she had Aunt Shalee to talk to. My aunt was a lot like my mother. She loved God and I'm sure she helped Rachel much more than I ever could. I was having a hard enough time on my own. But finally, things were getting a little easier with each passing day. I do think the trip to the river helped. I felt a little more relaxed than I usually did. The last thing I remembered before falling asleep was the time spent at the river making new friends. I couldn't explain it, but there was something very special about the three of us. It was like we had met each other before at another time. But I knew that couldn't be possible.

As sleep surrounded me, I fell deeper and deeper into that world of peace and rest . . . and dreams. I had numerous recurring dreams about water and its tremendous power for the past several years, and this night was no different. This time, I found myself walking on the shore of a large body of water, and the beach was covered with a dark, wet sand. As I looked out over the water, I saw a long, narrow, barren island, one with no trees, no vegetation, no life. The water was smooth as glass, no ripples, no movement at all, and it looked as if it would be hot to the touch. I reached down to place my fingers in the water, and I could see tiny wisps of steam lightly rising off the surface. The instant I touched the water with my finger, a shadow darkened everything around me. As I looked around and then up to the sky, I saw a huge wave of water, maybe a hundred feet high, ready to come crashing down over me. As I stood there looking, I could feel the mist from the white water at the wave's edge falling against my face. I took in my breath and closed my eyes; I braced myself for the impact and . . .

I never felt the water break over me. And in the next instant, I found myself walking along the shoreline, finding no debris, no timber, nothing. The water was back in the sea, showing no signs of having crested to such heights. But I saw before me something shining—something white. As I came nearer, I saw a robe lying on the beach. Against the dark beige color of the sand, this white cloth was almost blinding. I picked it up and saw that it was not soiled from the sand, and it was very warm to the touch. As I looked around with the robe in my hands, I realized I was looking for the children. Where were all the children?

I began crying when suddenly I awoke and felt tears running down my face. As I sat up in my bed, thinking about the dream, one that felt as if it had just happened, I remembered that I had had this same dream before. As I tried to remember more, I began to sense a fragrance in my room that was light and sweet. I knew the aroma from the vineyards. This was different. It was delightful and made me smile. Was I still dreaming? And as quickly as it came into my room, it was gone again. Just like my dream.

CHAPTER

The Unseen Miracle

I could hear Jonathan and Father loading even before the morning light could help them. After a while, I got up and got dressed, and I went out by the big tree where we have a water well. The colors of reds, oranges, and pinks were filling the sky as the sun peeked over the trees behind the house. I leaned against the tree, which must have been hundreds of years old, and I heard birds singing happily from the branches over my head.

I turned around when I heard Rachel come outside and saw she had her hands full of bread and fruit. Today would be a long day for me since she was going to Nazareth to help Aunt Shalee, and Father and Jonathan would be away. I thought about going with Rachel, but then I wanted to be home in case Stephen and Jesus came by on their way to the river again. They had mentioned it as a possibility.

"Aunt Shalee was running out of food at the house yesterday, so I thought I'd share some of ours with them," said Rachel, knowing that I would agree. We always had more than enough for us, and mother taught us that we should give, even if it's our last.

"Have a good day, Rach, and tell those kids I love them. I need to go with you next time so I can see them again. I miss the times we all had together," I said, knowing I could have gone with her that day. "Oh, and give a special hug to Donnie," I added.

Out of all the children my aunt had, Donnie was my favorite. Oh, I knew we weren't supposed to have favorites, but I did. And to see him, most people would think that he was the only one of her children who could not give back anything to those who loved him. How wrong they were.

Donnie was not always the way he was. Something happened when he was an infant, something that took away his ability to communicate, to take care of himself, to respond to those around him. No one ever talked about what actually happened. It was a secret my mother and Aunt Shalee knew. I'm not even sure my father knew; he never said anything. And now Aunt Shalee might be the sole owner of that information, and it was evident that no one should ever bring it up. She certainly didn't like to talk about it!

But there is still something about Donnie that touches me deep inside. He has beautiful blue eyes that would sometimes match the sky, and blond hair that curls around his face. He is one year older than I, but somehow he seems much younger. I love to sing to him because he loves music. He smiles and moves his hands to the beat when he hears a familiar song. And I always tell him I love him—because I do. And I tell him he is special—because he is. Sometimes he smiles when I talk to him and sometimes he doesn't. I wonder if God ever talks to him, and I wonder if Donnie can hear Him. I vowed right then to go with her the next time she went so I could see him again.

When Rachel left, I wandered about the house, wanting to hear my mother's voice, sometimes thinking I heard her singing out by the well. But the house was quiet with everyone gone. I think the silence made me miss her all the more.

My mind then drifted back to the dream I had the night before. I realized that it was almost exactly the same dream I often had, scene for scene. It was as if it really happened and my dreams and reality were somehow touching. But why had I been looking for children? I was always left with this uncomfortable feeling each time I had this particular dream. An uneasiness came over me as I stood in the middle of the room, lost in my thoughts.

"Sarina?" came the voice at the door, along with a steady knocking. "Are you in there?" I recognized the voice right away as it ripped me right back to reality. It was Stephen. They had decided to go back to the river and came by for me!

"Yes, I'm still here!" I answered. He opened the door, and there he stood with a basket full of fruit and a large loaf of bread.

"We're back! Think you might tear yourself away from your work and come with us?" Stephen asked.

"I'm free to go and stay all day," I said, looking past him. It was then I saw Jesus climbing the big tree out by the well. "What is he doing?" I asked as I stepped outside with Stephen.

"When we came up, he saw a little bird hopping around under the tree. We thought he might have fallen out of the nest, so Jesus decided to find the nest and put him back where he belongs."

As they looked up into the tree, Jesus had found the nest and was reaching way out on the limb to place the little bird back in it. When Jesus came down out of the tree, he waved to us and was starting back to the house when the bird fell out again. This time, Jesus picked him up and brought him into the house.

"He seems to be having a little trouble. I think he broke his wing this time," Jesus said as he sat down in the middle of the floor, setting the bird down in front of him. He gently stroked the wings of the bird and seemed to be fascinated with it. Then he picked it up and held it close to his heart.

"I think he also hurt his foot—he just keeps hopping around. Poor fellow isn't having a very good day, is he?"

"He is so good with animals," said Stephen. "Once I was with him when we came up on a wolf near a flock of sheep. I was so frightened that I started to run. But he told me to stop and just stand very still. He looked at the wolf right in the face and walked slowly right up to him. And the wolf just sat down and never growled, never tried to bite him or anything. He just has a way with animals."

"Well, it seems like the little guy likes you," I said to Jesus. "He keeps hopping up in your hand. Are you going to take him with us?"

"Actually, I think I'll try once more to put him back in the nest. Maybe this time his mother will keep him there until he gets well enough to fly away on his own," Jesus said as he continued to stroke its wing.

And we all walked out to the tree, with baskets and bread in hand, ready to go on down to the river for the day. Jesus climbed the tree once more and put the bird back in the nest. This time it looked like the bird was going to stay. So we walked away, down the road and around the curve, and the house, the well, and the old tree disappeared from our sight.

The wind began to blow a little harder and the limbs of the old tree were thrashing about when the little bird fell out of the nest once more. This time he just stood there in one place and a most astonishing thing happened. He waited for the next gust of wind to come and he hopped onto the breeze which lifted him so high, much higher than the old tree. And he began to fly on his own! This small miracle was part of the quiet that surrounded the well and the old tree—and no one knew what had really happened there . . . no one except the bird and the one who sent the breeze!

CHAPTER

A New Journey

The walk to the river was good for me. Instead of silence along the way, there was laughter and company, and by the time we reached the river, we were all hungry. As we sat there by the river's edge, eating and talking, it was clear that the three of us were becoming very close friends. We were all about the same age, lived fairly close to each other, and enjoyed talking about many different things. I learned a lot that day about the two of them. Really, I learned more about Stephen than I did about Jesus.

Stephen had been talking about a time in his life when he was too young to remember—a time when he lived near Jerusalem as a child in a town called Ramah. His mother had told him they lived there until he was three and then they moved to Cana. "We needed to be as far away from Jerusalem as we could be. The king at that time was a very evil man, and we only returned there for Passover feasts. But we would never live near there again!"

"What did the king do that made him so evil?" I asked, remembering how my own mother felt about that same part of the country.

"She never would tell me," Stephen said. "My father did tell me that those days in and around Jerusalem were very different than today. Strange things were happening in the night sky—and people were coming there from very far distances. The rumor was that the Messiah had been born and angels were appearing everywhere! I don't think my father knew what to tell me when I asked him if he believed that it was true. He just said that time would answer that question."

Jesus had been watching Stephen as he spoke and it was as if he had been there too. But he never said anything.

"My mother would tell me that same story, that important kings from far away places came to find the Messiah," I said. "Some people said he was born in Jerusalem, and others said He was born in Bethlehem. I'll always wonder what ever happened to that child—if there really was one born."

Jesus was deep in thought—remembering stories his mother told him—stories of kings that came to Bethlehem when he was born, stories of a star that led them there and how angels filled the sky one night with singing and rejoicing. He looked as though he wanted to say something, but then he just smiled.

Stephen didn't really give him time to speak anyway. "If it was the Messiah, then He would be about our age now. And very soon, He will be taking charge of this world and all the armies and powers of the earth will come under His control!"

Stephen was almost too exuberant, almost obsessed. "If it was not the Messiah, then I suppose we will continue to live under the rule of the Romans. Sometimes I want to disagree with God in the way He is carrying out His plan for Israel—and the time He is taking for it to happen. But then I realize that

God is not one to argue. He would probably just laugh and tell me to be patient or strike me down!"

His passion was one felt by many at that time. I wouldn't call him a true rebel, for it seemed as though he would never deliberately hurt anyone for any reason. But I could certainly see how his attitude easily mirrored those of a "zealot." That's what they were calling those Jewish men who were standing against the Roman government by aggressively taking action. The Roman influence was continually badgering our people. The nation of Israel was ready, waiting for God to make His move.

For the next few hours, we all talked about Jerusalem. I told them how much I had always wanted to go, but the stories from the past about wicked kings seemed to keep my family away. My father and Jonathan had been there only to deliver wine and to attend the traditional festivals required of every Jewish male.

Stephen described how crowded it was during the Passover Feast when thousands came into the city. The rabbis would gather in the temple, read the scriptures, and then discuss the meanings. Both Stephen and Jesus went there many times with their families.

A few hours into our conversation about Jerusalem, Jesus wanted to walk around down by the river bend, alone. It was then when Stephen told me much about this man who seemed very kind and very genuine, yet mysterious—very much to himself.

"He finds time in every day to be alone for a while. God is an important part of his life. He likes to spend time talking to Him," said Stephen as we watched Jesus walk away. "Over the years, our friendship has become so strong that he often shares with me things that are in his heart. He feels a certain strength growing inside him, and he is not absolutely sure yet what it means. But he knows that he will know when the time is right."

To know—what a gift. Mother had a way of knowing when something was right and it had a lot to do with God. Those conversations she had with Him must be what gave her the peace she had at the end. No wonder I was so drawn to Jesus. He was a lot like my mother!

Stephen took the opportunity to tell me more about Jesus. "That year when I first met him in Jerusalem, I remember a day when we had been sitting there at the temple for several hours, first with our fathers, and then the next day by ourselves. When Jesus had a question, he would ask it of the rabbis there and then a conversation would begin, one that showed what a deep understanding he had of the scriptures. All around him were amazed because of his age. He was speaking as a rabbi already, and he was only twelve years old!"

"Had he ever had any special teachings before this by his father?" I asked.

"No, that's what is so amazing. Joseph knew scriptures well enough, but he was not a rabbi and the knowledge that Jesus had acquired from his father was only a part of what he knew. It's really unexplainable. When he is talking about it, everyone is fixed on his every word. When you hear him teach, you know that what he is saying is true." Stephen was very impressed with Jesus.

"I know we really just met," said Stephen. "But I feel like I've known you for a long time. Maybe you could go with us when we go to Jerusalem next time. I would really like to show you around the city and we could all get to know each other more."

"I would like that. And I know I would like to know you better. You are so easy to talk to," I said.

CHAPTER 6

For the first time, I really looked into Stephen's eyes and found them warm and receptive. Inside, I felt a fluttering heart and wondered if it could be the first symptoms of a promising relationship. I had only known this man since yesterday, but something told me that what I was feeling was right. If it is, then my excitement made my heart flutter all the more!

CHAPTER

7

Truth Revealed

As time passed, regardless of *our* own needs or wants, the next two years did actually prove to be healing years as well as joyful ones. Rachel moved in with Aunt Shalee just a year after mother died. It was much easier for her to be there all the time with so many children to look after. There were times when I thought I might be more help there with them, but I knew I was no seamstress. And as the children grew older, they were able to help each other more and more.

Jonathan was dedicated to our father and he helped him in the vineyards from sun up to sun down. He chose not to look for a bride, at least not for now. Father was not the same since mother died. He just went through the motions and everyday living and working and didn't seem to find joy in anything.

As for me, I'm not really sure when it happened. Maybe it was that second day we spent down by the river when I felt the first of many stirrings in my heart when I was with Stephen. I had fallen in love with him. Oh, we hadn't talked about it a lot, but it was a feeling that we both had. I found a gentleness in him that I had only seen in one other man—in Jesus.

The three of us spent many times at the river. I loved to fish there, but I didn't like to touch the fish. I was a real inspiration! But with those guys around, I didn't have to worry. Stephen and I would spend a lot of time just talking about life in general. He was a very good man with some strong ideas, but it was his spirituality that drew me in to him.

I was close to Jesus, too, for he could warm your heart with just a glance, but it was clear from the beginning that his heart was not one to be captured and kept as one's own. He had a mission, and from what he had shared with Stephen and me, it was one of great importance. He had been talking about going away for a long while now, and just last week, he told us that the time was very close.

"Why do you feel that you must go away?" I asked him one day when just he and I were together at the river. Stephen was helping my father and would join us later.

"Life is very busy. We do what we must do to help others and keep peace among us. But the time comes when we must draw away from the world and listen to the Father. That becomes harder and harder as I become attached to the people around me. The closer I get to people, especially you and Stephen, the harder it is for me to pull away. I need to focus on whatever mission the Father has for me. I trust I will discover answers by drawing away for a while."

"We will miss you. The three of us have become like family, Jesus. Will you be gone for long?" I asked.

"I do not know," he said. "But I do know you and I know Stephen. He has been my best friend for many years, Sarina, and in the past couple of years, I have seen the way he looks at you. I have heard him talk about you. Even though he may not say it, he is in love with you."

"Oh I love him, too, Jesus. I just hoped and prayed he felt the same way. Why do you think he doesn't ever say it?" I asked him.

"Some things are just understood. They don't need words. Your spirit and his know what's going on. In your heart, the fluttering you feel is that spirit just waiting for the time it can fully embrace Stephen's, and the two of you can become one. Love is like that."

"Well, that's worth waiting for—as long as it takes! So what about you?" I asked. "Do you think you'll ever find love like that?"

"I don't know, Sarina. Love takes many forms. But I do know this. I am here for a purpose." Jesus hesitated for a moment before he spoke to me again.

"What I'm about to share with you, Sarina, is going to be pretty hard to believe. But you trust me, don't you?"

For a moment, my heart sank. I felt a little scared and I wasn't sure why. I trusted this man with my life. He was a true friend and I would believe anything he said.

"Of course, I trust you," I said. "What is this about?"

"Do you remember those stories you heard when you were young about the baby born in Bethlehem and the angels appearing to shepherds?" he said, his eyes sparkling.

"Yes, I do. We talked about that when we first met. Does this have anything to do with your leaving?" I asked him, a little confused.

"I don't remember very much at all, but there are times when way down deep inside my memories, I can see a bright light pulsating like a star, and I can see many faces looking down at me. My mother tells of an incredible story about kings from the east visiting, and shepherds who came to see what was going on. I asked my mother why my birth was so important and she said that . . ."

Jesus paused for a moment. He had tears in his eyes. Then he looked straight into mine and said, "She said I was born to be the Messiah. My birth was foretold in scripture."

I found myself holding my breath as I listened to him. What was he saying? I knew him well enough to know he would not make this up. What has happened to him?

Jesus continued. "Sarina, I know this sounds incredible, but the miracles that happened over twenty-seven years ago were part of a plan that God has made for mankind. Over the past few years, I have known that my life was already directed by God's will. I know I have a choice. And I know faith will make me strong, and I will have the right answers I need when the Father wants to tell me. But there is so much to ask, so much to know. I need some time apart to prepare for what I already know to be my mission."

I wasn't sure if I heard everything he said—did he say the word *Messiah*? I wondered if he had told Stephen because he had been looking for and talking about . . . *I couldn't even imagine it. . .*about the *Messiah* coming for as long as I've known him and before. I remember when he said the Messiah would come with a huge army with power and strength! Did he really believe Jesus could be the One? Surely they had talked about it, as close as they were. I finally was able to simply utter, "I don't know what to say."

Jesus looked away, drew in a deep breath, and then said, "I want you to know that I have entrusted you with this because you have your mother's gift. You don't think you do, but you just haven't used it. Your dreams are right before you. Reaching out to understand them is the first step to the gift. Ask the Father to help you, Sarina, and you will know the truth about who I am."

"Have you talked to Stephen about this?" I managed to ask, still awed by all he had said and not really listening to what he said about "knowing the truth."

"Stephen and I have talked about this and much more. He knows we are sharing it now because he wanted me to be the one to tell you. But I must tell you that he is not sure that I am who I say I am." Jesus said. "He wants me to stay here, in Nazareth, and can't seem to understand why I must leave."

"But the two of you—you are still friends?" I asked, afraid that this might come between them.

"Oh yes, we will always be best friends," said Jesus. "And he will eventually believe this when God gives him the knowledge he needs to see clearly."

"I'm not sure what I think," I said. "It seems so unbelievable!"

"This life I have always known will be hard to leave. Because I know I will never be back to live here and it can never be the same. But my friendship with you and Stephen will never change. I'll carry you with me wherever I go. Someday, we will all know the truth."

Uncertainty is hard to swallow. This was a world-changing event he wanted me to accept. I wasn't sure I could believe it. And on that very day, he left.

CHAPTER

Nothing but the Truth

How do you measure time except by those things that happen in your life that are unforgettable? Each night in the months that followed, I would lie awake and think about my dream, but it would never come. I remembered what Jesus said like it was yesterday. "Your dreams are right before you—reaching out to understand them is the first step to the gift." He couldn't possibly know about my dreams. But maybe his mention of it caused me to remember it again and again.

I never shared that dream with Stephen. Oh, I shared other dreams: how I wanted to marry and have children. Stephen had a special place in my heart. Nothing would ever be able to replace that love I felt for him. But this dream was my own. And my questions were always with me. It was something I had to personally work out for myself. I needed to find the answers.

Stephen and I tried to talk about Jesus and why he had to leave. The first few weeks after he left, Stephen was hurt. He pleaded with him not to go. He even offered to go with him.

But Jesus would not agree. When I began talking about missing him, Stephen would change the subject.

I remember the day Jesus's father, Joseph, died. It was two years after Jesus left. Stephen had come to Nain to tell me, and I never saw him cry until that day. Not even when Jesus left.

"You would think he would keep in touch with his own family!" cried Stephen, angered and full of grief. "Why in the last two years hasn't he come back home? I don't understand. I just don't understand!"

Joseph had been a second father to Stephen. He taught him most of what he knew about carpentry. None of this made any sense to him. Where was his sense of family? Where was Jesus?

I tried to comfort him for I couldn't bear to see him cry. He was always so strong.

"Stephen, listen to me for a moment. Do you remember when you and Joseph talked about Jesus a few months after he left? Joseph told you that what Jesus had said was true. All of it. Even Mary tried to help you understand this 'thing,' this 'event' that was beginning to happen in our lifetime. Joseph told you that Mary was especially chosen to be his mother. It was God, Stephen, who made that choice. That's when I finally began to understand that maybe what Jesus said was believable. Mary and Joseph were there from the beginning."

Stephen's tear-filled eyes looked straight into mine. "If that is true, don't you know what it will mean for him? The scriptures are very clear."

I wasn't sure I really understood what Stephen meant about the scriptures. But I did know that he was now beginning to believe that what Jesus had told him was true.

I began to notice a change in Stephen around that time. He was meeting with a few men in town who were really upset with the Roman soldiers taking our taxes and animals and the cruelty they showed our people. They met more often than they used to, and were becoming a lot more boldly protective than normal. I wondered if he thought that if Jesus was the Messiah, he would come and lead them in battle against the Romans and take back their land. I just didn't see Jesus doing that. I wish he was still around to talk to. I really miss that.

CHAPTER

9

Life Goes On

Things were going well with Aunt Shalee and her family. She had been spending time with Joda, who was introduced to her as "a fisherman" from Capernaum. He had relatives in Nazareth and they met at a wedding there for one of his cousins.

When I first saw Joda, he reminded me of John, one of Jesus's strange-looking cousins whom I only met once. John had come to see Mary when Joseph died, but he did not have any news about Jesus.

Aunt Shalee planned to marry Joda and then move to Capernaum with all the children. If I had not seen him with Donnie, I would have been saddened about their leaving. But one evening while I was visiting my aunt, Joda was there. I watched him as he talked to Donnie. It was as if Donnie could hear and understand everything Joda said to him. When I saw Donnie smile as only he can, I saw a small tear form in the corner of Joda's eye, and Joda smiled back as big as his face would let him. I saw love come from that man, and my heart went out to the whole family.

CHAPTER 9

I asked Rachel if she planned to return home after the marriage, and her answer surprised me.

"I think I'll stay here in Nazareth. There's a lot here to stay for."

"And why would you want to stay here without family, without eight children around you, without—you've met someone, haven't you?" I said.

"Do you remember meeting Samuel?" she said. "Well, we have been seeing each other for a while now. He is going to talk to father soon and ask that we be married. Aunt Shalee gave me her house for my own because of all my hard work."

And she went on for several minutes about what her new plans were. So there she was—Rachel bubbling on and on about where she knew she belonged. And Aunt Shalee making a new life for herself and her family. And then there was me.

Things with Stephen were so good. We shared good times and sad times, and we really became closer than I ever thought possible. I remember one evening when we were at the river, he asked me a question.

"Do you remember the first time we met?"

"We were sitting by the tree at the river. I remember it well," I said.

Stephen took a long deep breath and said, "The second day, when we were talking about going to Jerusalem, I told you I would like to know more about you. I looked deep into your eyes for the first time and I liked what I saw. You have a gentle spirit and my heart began to race. I think I fell in love with you at that moment, Sarina. I do love you, with all my heart."

"I know, Stephen. In my heart, I've known it all along. I love you, too, with all I have to give," I said.

Jesus was right. I did *know*. I just had to let God say when the time was right.

Stephen had a pleased look on his face because of what he had heard.

"I would love to have you as my wife, Sarina. Will you say yes?" he asked.

"Yes, yes, yes!" I said. And we embraced and kissed. At that moment, I was the happiest I think I've ever been. I was riding the top of that hundred foot wave in my dream!

We talked about a life together and our dreams and wishes, and nothing could take away our joy (nothing except not ever hearing from Jesus). I didn't know it, but Stephen had been building a house for us for a while now. He had even talked to my father about our marriage. If I could just tell my mother! Is this the "find him" she was talking about? Maybe part of my puzzle is finally solved.

CHAPTER

10

The Unveiling

It's been three years since Jesus first left, and I still think about him every day. Even though I didn't understand all that was happening, he was a part of my family. And even as months had turned into years without him around, I never forgot the sound of his voice or the blueness of his eyes.

My dreams were back. Nothing ever changed. It always ended the same, with the white robe on the sand, and I never found the children. It's haunting me now because I feel as though I should know what it means. Maybe it's all just a dream with no significant meaning. Only, why would I keep dreaming the same thing over and over again?

I still never shared the dream with Stephen. We were planning our wedding. It was only four weeks away now, and Rachel's wedding was in two weeks. She and Samuel were perfect for each other: she talked, and he listened!

Aunt Shalee and Joda were married last spring in Capernaum. I only wish mother could have been here. There had been a lot of sorrow in my aunt's past with the death of her husband and her sister. She was due this happiness in her life. And it looks like she finally got it!

I had spent most of the day before the wedding with Donnie. Even though I did not see him often, I was going to miss him. He was always the same. My heart ached inside for him because he could not talk back to me. And I knew he had so much to say. Sometimes, when he looked at me, it was as if I knew he wanted to tell me something very important. But he would just smile and then look off into the distance.

When all the celebration had settled down, I took Donnie with me about a mile away from the city. There was a place on higher ground where we could see a far distance. It was quiet and peaceful, and we could even see the Sea of Galilee glistening on the horizon. I began to sing to him and that smile filled his face once again.

What had happened to this man, this boy who was just a little older than I? He was once whole, and then something tragic happened. Why wouldn't anyone talk about it? And now that they were leaving, I may never know. Why would I need to? God loves him anyway. And why am I so obsessed by it?

As we sat there on that hillside, I talked to God. I hadn't been doing that as often lately, and it was good to be with Him again. I said a prayer especially for Donnie, thanking God that He loves us all, no matter what we say or do, or how we look or act.

"Please keep him in your special care, because somehow, I know he loves you too. Maybe he can't tell you, and then maybe he can. Talk to him, God, and let him know you are there. This child of yours needs to feel your love so he doesn't feel lost. He is precious and I love him too. Keep him safe."

Knowing it would be a long time before I saw him again, I didn't feel guilty spending so much time with him alone that day. We talked about so many things—the birds and how they are dressed by God, the trees and how they are so free, their limbs dancing to the wind as it blows swiftly across the land. I even told him about the dreams, perhaps just to hear it aloud instead of holding it inside. Donnie would listen, and I am not sure he understood, but you could see through to his spirit, and our time together was good.

When we got back to the house, Aunt Shalee called me into her part of the house. "You are so good for Donnie. I am sure he is going to miss you very much."

"He is so special, Aunt Shalee. I'll miss him too," I said. "I'll just have to visit often."

I watched her as she stared into the next room at Donnie. Tears began to form in the corners of her eyes. It was almost as if she wanted to run away and hide. But she turned to me, looking through those tears, and embraced me. I wanted to ask her all about his past. But I didn't have to.

"I've never told you what I hold in my heart. The only ones who know were those who were there and old enough to understand. You have always loved him, Sarina. You deserve to know the truth."

I could see she wanted to let go of all the sadness she felt, and I wasn't sure I wanted to hear it anymore.

"When Donnie was almost two years old, he was a beautiful, healthy boy who was so gifted and active that it was hard to keep up with him. Being my firstborn, he was watched over so carefully and all my attention was given to him. If only we had left the city when . . ."

She had to stop a moment and regain composure.

"Well, we thought about moving away from Ramah, which is where we lived, a year earlier when your uncle came back from Jerusalem one day with news about his relatives from Nazareth. They needed help and wanted us to come live there for a while. But he decided that moving at that time was not the right choice. Then one year later . . ."

Aunt Shalee paused. Even though it was so many years ago, I could see it was so traumatic that she could not finish.

"You don't have to tell me, Aunt Shalee, if it hurts that much. I don't have to know."

"But I want to. Something inside me is saying that when I tell you, there is a healing that will finally begin in my life. The king of that day was so afraid that someone else would take away his throne that he became obsessed with finding the child that so many had talked about. It was said that the Messiah had been born somewhere near Jerusalem, and that the big beautiful star we saw at night was marking the place of his birth. After this king thought about how he might lose his throne, he commanded that every baby who had just recently been born, up to the age of two years old, be killed by his soldiers! So they came with swords and knives, and they came in the night when we had no warning. I heard screams down the way, and when I looked out my window, it was so dark, I couldn't see what was happening. I rushed to the doorway and your uncle was ahead of me. While we were looking out the doorway, I heard Donnie scream from his bed. One of the soldiers had crawled through the open window and had taken him away! I ran after them, but he mounted his horse and as I watched them round the corner, I saw Donnie fall from the horse and hit the rocks near the water well. The soldier just went on. I'm sure he thought Donnie was dead. He fell on his head, and it was all covered with blood. As I rushed to him, Donnie was lifeless. He had also been pierced in two places near the heart. All I could hear was screams and crying as I saw the children of Ramah lying in the street, dying. It was just . . . unbelievable. I carried Donnie back to the house and I cried until I had no more tears. I cleaned him up and put him to bed. He was still alive, breathing rather slowly, but nonetheless, breathing. He stayed in the same position for three weeks before waking, never turning, never crying. And from that day on, he was never the same. All the energy had been taken out of him. His very life was stolen by that soldier. And I know I should be grateful that he is still alive, but is he? What does he know? What does he hear? Does God know about Donnie? I've asked myself those questions so many times. And your mother is the very one who said I should share this with you when the time was right. She knew you were closer to Donnie than any of the rest of us. I don't have answers for what happened. But she convinced me not to blame God. She told me to just love him as he is because God does. And you have always loved him Sarina, just as he is."

I didn't know how to take all this in. Such tragedy was never even imagined, and even though I had heard stories about this, I never thought them to be true. So many children, so many deaths, all gone in an instant. Poor Donnie. He was so young, he probably doesn't even know what happened to him.

"I never knew any of this," I said. Embracing her, I smiled and said, "We both know that Donnie is very special. I will always cherish my love for him."

We talked for a while longer as I helped her pack her things to take to Capernaum the next day. It felt good to grow closer to Aunt Shalee and despite knowing the details of Donnie's past, there was a kind of peace that came over me. We all stayed overnight, talking, laughing, singing, and having a wonderful time. I will truly miss them all. Especially Donnie. And Capernaum is not so far away.

That night, I walked outside Aunt Shalee's house looking up into the sky. I thought about all the things she had told me. I cried for Donnie and all the other children lost at the hand of a cruel king. I could almost hear the cries of the mothers who watched their children die before their very eyes. I sat down next to an old tree that reminded me of home. Then I thought about Jesus and where he fit into all this. Where was he when the soldiers came to kill the babies? Deep in thoughts, I must have fallen asleep. I felt a shadow come over me and as I looked up to the sky, I felt a mist on my face from the white water at the wave's edge. I held my breath for what seemed like an eternity for I knew I was going under. But it didn't happen. Or at least, I didn't feel it happen. Where are they? Where are the children? Where is Donnie? Where is the child he once was? And in my hand was a brilliant white robe, warm and reassuring. And I remember waking up and walking into the house with a sweet fragrance lingering in the air, knowing just a little more about dreams and why they seem so real. Life is real. And this part of the puzzle is one I wish I had left alone.

CHAPTER

11

Reunited and It Feels Good

Rachel's wedding day was only two weeks away. I don't think I've ever seen her so bubbly. They were going to settle in a nearby town called Cana because Samuel had relatives there. My father instantly liked Samuel. He was a hard worker, and from the first minute they were introduced, they seemed to have a lot to talk about. And Jonathan liked him too. It was just like having a brother. And I really think Jonathan needed that.

Rachel told me she wanted to have so many children, they would have a hard time keeping track of them! She had asked me if I wanted the house in Nazareth. I told her to give it to someone else or sell it because Stephen was building our house and had been working hard on it. He was such a good carpenter. He was so proud of his work, and it was so beautiful with so much room inside. He wanted us to be married there in our new house, and he was trying to finish it before *our* wedding day.

I'll never forget the day he first took me there. As I turned a corner and looked just past the trees, I saw it! The house was larger than normal, and the workmanship was beautiful. When you entered the front double doorway, it had an open courtyard with three rooms off to the left side. The craftsmanship was absolutely stunning. On the right, he had a workshop where he could keep his tools. There were stairs in the back that went up on the roof. He even laid stones around the doorways. It looked like a palace to me!

"I don't know what to say, Stephen. It's absolutely magnificent!"

"It's something Joseph would have been proud of," said Stephen. "He taught me so much—I truly miss him. And I miss Jesus."

It had been a long time since we last saw Jesus, but Stephen had been talking to Jesus's mother, and it seemed to help him understand why he had to leave. We talked about him now and even though we didn't understand why he left or where he went, we did understand his love for us. Stephen's answer was that we would just wait and see what happens.

"Father and Jonathan are planning on bringing the wine for Rachel's wedding the day before," I said. "There will be so many people at their wedding. . ."

Just then, a voice called from outside the house. "Is there a Stephen or a Sarina here?"

We looked at each other with a puzzled look. No one knew we had come here to the house. But the voice did seem somewhat familiar.

Stephen answered, "Yes. Here in the back of the house."

"I understand there is to be a wedding here this summer, and I didn't get my invitation," the voice said.

When Stephen saw who it was, he ran to him!

"Jesus!" Stephen shouted. "I can't believe it's you!" It seemed that all the doubts about who he was seemed to vanish as they embraced.

"It's me. How are you two doing?" Jesus said as he came over to me and gave me the biggest hug ever.

"Everything is great with us. Oh, how we've missed you!" I said with big tears in my eyes. "It's been so long."

"I know it has," he said. "Time is such a valuable gift. But I haven't forgotten either one of you. I have missed you both."

"There isn't a day that has gone by that I haven't thought about you. Sarina and I are so glad you are back," said Stephen. "How did you know where we were?"

"I went by my mother's house before coming out here. She told me where I could find you. We had a long talk, and she mentioned how you didn't understand why I didn't come when my father died. Actually, I did come, but no one knew I was here—only mother. She and I talked for hours about his loyalty and his courage in the face of danger. He faced many trials that most other men will never encounter. He was a good father and I learned much from him."

Jesus was somehow different. I couldn't quite put my finger on it. He always spoke softly and that hadn't changed at all. But he looked different. He looked older. Wiser. But his eyes had not changed at all. I could still look into them and see way beyond the present.

"Your family was so loving and supportive of your mother. And many friends and neighbors came by to help. Joseph was well thought of in Nazareth," I said. "But why didn't you want us to see you?"

"I was discovering so much about myself about the past, the present, and my future." Jesus answered. "It was just not a good time for explanations."

"What about your future?" asked Stephen. "You are back now for good, right?" He asked the question, knowing full well the answer before Jesus spoke.

"For a few weeks at least!" Jesus said. "Right now, I'd like to talk about you two! Someone told me about your wedding! Stephen, you really are blessed. Sarina is so right for you! And you, Sarina! It takes a good woman to put up with a man like him!"

We laughed and joked around for a while. Then we showed him the house and he was very impressed. Of course, he told Stephen that if he had been here to help, it would have looked so much better, and they could have done this and that, but it was all in fun. He really knew Stephen had gone all out to make it the best he had ever done.

And we spent the next two weeks together, Stephen, Jesus, and me. When the subject would come up about the future, Jesus was strangely quiet. He would never say anything about where he was going or what he was going to do. He had mentioned that he spent some time with John, his cousin (the strange one). But most of the time he said he had been on his own.

On the day of Rachel's wedding, my father and Jonathan were late. They had been unable to bring wine in the day before because of the bad weather. So they decided to bring the wine the morning of the wedding. My father came, but he was feeling sick. They weren't able to load as much as they wanted, but they were sure it would be enough.

The wedding was beautiful. And I have never seen so many people! Samuel knew everyone in the surrounding towns. Aunt Shalee and Joda were there with the family, and all of Samuel's relatives were there, (he had a *big* family). The party was everywhere—inside Samuel's house, outside the house, in the fields, on the roadway—and it was exciting. Jesus was the happiest I think I've ever seen him. He danced and talked with everyone. What I remember most is when he went over to Donnie. He whispered something to him and Donnie's eyes seemed to light up. I know in my heart Donnie heard him. And maybe even understood.

Toward the end of the day, a strange thing happened. Rachel and I were in the house when I remember looking out the window seeing my father, Samuel, Aunt Shalee, and Mary, Jesus's mother, all huddled together, murmuring and gesturing. I called out to Stephen who went over to find out what was wrong. The next thing I knew, Mary called Jesus over. Rachel and I started over when Stephen came up to us.

"Everything is fine, Sarina," said Stephen. "They are just a little low on wine. And a few of the guests were asking for more."

"Oh no! I know my father must feel terrible. There are so many people here. What are they going to do?" I asked.

"I'm not sure," said Stephen. "But Mary said she has an idea."

Stephen, Rachel, and I went over to Mary, who was talking to Jesus.

"You can do this," she said.

"Mother, it is not yet time," answered Jesus.

What were they talking about? Not yet what time? That didn't make any sense.

"It *is* time, Jesus! There is always a beginning," said Mary.

"Do as my son says," said Mary to the servants.

Jesus hesitated for just a moment, and then went over to the servants. I stood there and watched them as they listened to Jesus and poured water from one jug to another. Then it happened! The water began to turn colors—first a light pink, then darker, and then—it turned to the color of wine! I couldn't believe my eyes! But I saw it happen. Stephen looked at me and then at Jesus.

My father came up to see if they found more wine, and Stephen gave him a cup of the new wine. He tasted it.

"This wine is better than the first. More wine for all," my father announced. And it was the best wine we had ever tasted. "I'm not even sure this is *my* wine. It is perfect!"

"Uh, Jesus. Could I see you for a minute—outside?" asked Stephen. Jesus just smiled and followed Stephen outside, and looked back over his shoulder at me, with a smile from ear to ear.

Mary came up to me after a few minutes had passed. I must have had a funny look on my face for she said, "Sarina, it's okay. You of all people must know that Jesus is special. This is only the beginning."

And that is the last time she spoke about the miracle I saw on my sister's wedding day.

CHAPTER

12

Coming to Terms

Later that evening, Stephen was quiet. He didn't say anything about his talk with Jesus when they went outside at Rachel's wedding. And he always talked to me about things like that. We shared everything, all our thoughts, all our dreams. Well, that wasn't entirely true. I never shared my "special" dream with anyone, except Donnie. Jesus and I never talked about it specifically, but he knew something about it. Why couldn't I share it with Stephen? I trusted him with everything. I loved him with all my heart, but I just couldn't talk about the dream.

The day after Rachel's wedding, we all went to the river, Stephen, Jesus, and I. We talked about old memories for a while, but the conversation eventually came around to what we had witnessed at the wedding.

"Sarina, I've already talked to Stephen about the wedding yesterday and the wine. . ."

Jesus must have seen a funny look on my face because he hesitated.

"There is not an easy way to explain this. My mother asked me to help your father by providing more wine. So I did."

Inside, I was shaking. I looked over at Stephen, and he was deep in thought, looking out over the water.

"I thought . . . oh, I don't know what I thought, or what I think. I'm so confused!" I said.

"While I was away, Sarina," Jesus said, "I learned more about who I really am. And I have so much to do and so little time to do it. There will be many things you will see happen, and you will not want to believe it at first. But you will come to know in your heart what the truth really is. I have a message for the world to hear. And many will hear and believe and others will never believe. It will be hard for you to understand, but I know that you will know in your heart what the truth really is. Remember what you told me about your mother's last words? She said, 'He's here.' She already knew in her spirit that you would someday witness events that will change the course of mankind. We have shared much as friends, you, Sarina, and you, Stephen. I will always cherish our years together. Please believe me when I tell you this. For things will now happen that may keep us apart. I want you to know that I am doing my Father's will."

Stephen stood, looked straight into Jesus's eyes, and turned away, walking the river's edge, lost in his own thoughts. I started to go to him, but Jesus stopped me.

"Just give him time, Sarina. He is having a hard time accepting the truth. I was the kid he ran around with in Nazareth. We did everything together. This is too unbelievable for him. He needs time."

"I want to believe you, Jesus. There has always been something very special about you. But what does it all mean? I don't understand," I said.

CHAPTER 12

"Maybe it's like your dream, Sarina. When the wave breaks on the shore, the children are lost. But only for a while, for then they will be found. I am the breaking wave, the mist you feel upon your face. The children are like Donnie—broken, not whole. When they are found, they will become whole once again."

I couldn't say anything. No one knew about my dream. But he knew. I didn't know whether to laugh or cry, to be happy or sad. Jesus just embraced me and let me take it all in. How could he know about my dream? The children are like Donnie? Lost but found? Because of him? I had a lot of thinking to do, but somehow I knew part of me was beginning to understand. Jesus had come into the world for a purpose. Mother knew this before she died, but I never thought I had that "knowing" in my heart. The Messiah has come to find us—God's children who were lost and broken—to save us. But how would he do that? What did he mean when he said "things may happen that will keep us apart?" I couldn't ever let go of this dear friend who knew so much about life and love and about me. What was going to happen?

We spent the rest of that day together, for we all knew it would never be the same for us again. And Stephen was still far away, for something inside his heart told him what Jesus said was true. But his head told him it was impossible and he was not willing to let go of his brother.

After hearing those words of revelation, how does one come to terms with what's real and what's not? And selfish me! I thought the "He's here" from my mother's lips was all about me and my husband to be. But it was deeper. My dreams are deeper than I was willing to look. God is the wave and the mist that comes over us to protect and save us. How could my friend Jesus who played with the little bird, who made wine at my sister's wedding, be my friend, be my God?

CHAPTER
13

The Wedding

Our wedding was one filled with mixed emotions. It was joyous seeing a smile on Stephen's face again. Having Jesus there at this important time in our life was such a blessing, but I think we both knew that it wouldn't be long before we would lose him again. And we were right. Jesus left the day after our wedding came to a close. It was like he knew if he stayed longer, it would be harder for him to leave.

One thing was for certain. We did not run out of wine! Father made sure this time we had more than enough. He started on it a week before because he was still feeling poorly.

All the family was there, Samuel and Rachel, Aunt Shalee and Joda, and all the kids. Stephen's family was even bigger than Samuel's! He had many aunts and uncles who had many children. It was such a beautiful way to begin our marriage, with lots of love surrounding us.

We had days of good food and wine, dancing and gifts. And then more wine. The ceremony was something I will never forget. We spoke our own words to each other, and he promised to pick me up when I fall, to laugh with me, to cry with me, and to love me forever. I will honor him and always love him as he is a part of my heart forever.

Mary came. I had come to love her as part of the family. Since Jesus had been away for so long and Joseph was gone, I couldn't help but feel how alone she must have been. When I thought about all she knew about Jesus, I marveled at her composure. She was so patient and so gracious. From his very birth, she knew how important his life would be. How could she keep it all in?

When I asked her if she knew where Jesus had been all this time, she just confirmed that he was not revealing that to her either.

"He's been pretty quiet about his whereabouts," Mary said. "The only news I heard was through Elizabeth. Her son, John, saw him at the Jordan River. Jesus went out alone into the wilderness for a very long time, but he told John that he would be back. Before he left, John baptized him! And the witnesses there marveled at what they saw. It was like the heavens opened up and a thundering voice came over them. It said, 'This is my beloved son and I am so pleased with him!' I know His time has come, Sarina, and my heart is getting heavy."

I didn't ask her any more questions for I knew she had much more on her mind than she was willing to share. I didn't want to go that direction, not at my wedding.

As I think back to that day Stephen and I met; I can see why God made me wait for him. I fell in love with his spirit. There was something down deep inside of him that would never change. His love for me mirrors God's love, and I felt safe in his arms. I just knew he would always love me. Even in the bad times. But these were the good times. And I was going to enjoy them while I could!

CHAPTER

Mourning in the Night

It hardly seems possible that Rachel and Samuel have been married almost a year now and already have a little girl. Rachel was meant to be a mother. After all, she had a lot of experience with my aunt's children.

We saw Rachel and Samuel, and Leah (named after my mother), at least once a week. But it had been a while since we had seen my aunt and her family. So, Stephen and I decided to go to Capernaum.

The last time we visited, they were moving to a new house near the water. With Joda being a fisherman, he spent most of his time by the sea. And Donnie loved the water.

One of his sisters, Mira, would take him down to see Joda come in with the other fishermen. They would spend the day there and everyone along the shore got to know Donnie and Mira. In fact, when we arrived there, that's where we went first. And there they were. Donnie's face lit up with a big smile as he saw us approaching.

"I have missed you so much," I said as I gave Donnie and Mira a big hug. "Where is everyone?"

Mira pointed out to the water and said, "They went fishing with Peter. He's the one fisherman down here that usually catches the most fish, but he's real moody. I really love Joda and he's a great husband for mother, but Peter is a bad influence. He always loses his temper over the little things. Yesterday they went out all day and didn't catch anything. When they came back in, there was a man on shore who told him he should go back out and try again."

"Did he go?" asked Stephen.

"Not without a fight! He said they were tired and it was no use trying again. There were no fish out there. His friends tried to get him to do it. They had been listening to this man they called Rabbi and they believed most everything he said."

"So he didn't want to even try?" I said.

"Oh, he went. He was flinging the rope around, rocking the boat, and all the Rabbi did was just smile. They were only gone a short time when we saw them coming back. I just knew Peter had offended the Rabbi, but when they pulled into dock, the boat was filled with fish, from stern to bow! And the look on Peter's face was shock! He didn't say a word!"

"You mean, they brought in a bunch of fish because the Rabbi told them it would happen?" I asked.

"I've never seen anything like it," said Mira. "It was a miracle if ever I've seen one!"

"What happened after that?" asked Stephen.

"His other friends on the boat, James, John, and Andrew, followed the Rabbi. I'm not sure where they went. But Peter is just being quiet. He doesn't want to talk about it. Maybe Joda can fill us in when he gets back," said Mira.

It was just a few minutes later when we heard loud voices. We saw an old man running around, crying out that someone had just healed him. He had been crippled since birth and this man had touched his legs and made them well. Most everyone around didn't believe his story, but he urged them all to come and listen to the Rabbi. He would be just outside the city tomorrow.

"I'd like to go, Stephen," I said. "There's something about what the man said. I'd like to hear more from this Rabbi."

"We can go. But for now, why don't you go on to the house with Mira and Donnie. Your aunt is expecting you. I think I'll wait for Joda and talk to some of the other fishermen." Stephen had something on his mind. But I wasn't going to ask him what I thought I knew already.

Later that night at my aunt's house, when we were all asleep and it was quiet, we heard a knock on the door. Joda got up to see who it was, and Stephen followed. I could hear low voices trying to be quiet, but there was an urgency in the tone. Something had happened.

The door to our room opened up, and Stephen came to my side of the bed. "Sarina," he said. "I need you to wake up."

"I'm awake," I said. "What's going on?"

"It's your father. Jonathan found him in the vineyard today. He said it looks like he just lay down and went to sleep. He's . . . passed away. I'm so sorry." He held me tight and cried with me just like he said he would. "We'll leave for Nain at dawn."

I couldn't believe it. My father passed away? We just saw him three days ago, and he was fine. I began to recall all the things I said to him that day, my last words to him, he was such a hard worker, I had asked him to slow down. He didn't have to take on so much extra work. Jonathan was there to help.

Jonathan. I began to think about how he must be feeling. He would be so lost without Father. I remembered how I felt when mother died and how that was such a hard time for me. Going back to sleep now was impossible. My mind was going in a thousand different directions. I began to pack the few things we brought with us. Short visit this time. Death comes at unexpected times. But even when you expect it, does it really matter? The loss is the same. The emptiness is the same.

Rachel and Leah were already there when we arrived. Samuel was delivering wine for Jonathan. There were orders to fill in Jerusalem, and Samuel had to go there anyway. So he asked Jonathan if he could do this for him. Leah was sitting in Rachel's lap, and her eyes lit up when she saw us. She loved her grandfather. Oh, to be innocent again. She called him Popo and just laughed when he picked her up. Father said she had the eyes of Mother. And she was already singing all the time.

Jonathan and I talked for a long time about Father and how he was never really happy after mother died. His entire life was devoted to her. After Leah was born last year, he seemed to be happier than he had been in a long time, but I knew it was because there was a "Leah" back in our lives again. I believe he never really accepted her death gracefully. I asked Jonathan if they ever talked about her.

"Never," he said. "If I ever started to say anything about mother, he just changed the subject. But on the day he died, he was talking to her in the vineyard. I could hear him almost whispering. He was calling out her name over and over. I truly believe he died of a broken heart because he missed her so much."

Jonathan looked so tired. "We really need to get some rest. When will Samuel be back?" I asked.

"The trip normally takes three full days, but after talking with Stephen, he thinks there is a storm between here and Jerusalem. He might be delayed."

Sleep didn't come easy that night. The sound of light raindrops was soothing, but the mind is not easy to calm down.

As morning came, I was still awake, listening to the distant thunder.

Stephen was lying next to me. I was so blessed to have him. He had been there for me as I cried for my father. It was hard to get close to a father who wouldn't let you in. But he was the one who began this family, along with my mother. And I loved them both dearly.

So I whispered into the night, "I love you both so much. You have given us a family and taught us what love is. Sleep on into the night precious ones."

CHAPTER

15

When You're Right, You're Wrong

It was raining that day, and many friends and mourners were there. We all ate, talked about father, cried, and went through all the motions required of the family. It never feels real when it's happening. Only when it's over does reality appear.

Jonathan decided to continue with the vineyard. He was doing most of the work anyway, and it was his very life. I was almost afraid that he would be like father and become an introvert. He was always so much like a baby brother. But over the last couple of years, he had changed. That day, he did tell me that he had met someone. She was a lot like mother, but he felt his first responsibility was with father. So he had not pursued the relationship. Things were different now. He thought he might have to give that a little more thought. And my little brother had grown up right before my very eyes.

The one who would miss "Popo" the most was not Leah, but Rachel. I was surprised because I thought it might be Jonathan.

Rachel was always happy, but now she seemed depressed. She told me that father was her link to our mother. When I told her I didn't understand, she explained it to me.

"Mother was so committed to father and loved him so much that everything she did honored him. And he did the same for her. Their marriage was so blessed that I find it hard to measure up to it. With both gone now, that example of pure love is gone too. His death has put them both out of our lives now. I love Samuel with all my heart and he loves me. But we do have our differences. I never saw our parents have a cross word with each other."

"They did have a wonderful marriage," I said. "But Rachel, their differences were between the two of them. They had no reason to let us see that. Keep the memory of their marriage and love in your heart. That's where they belong now. And no one can ever take that away!"

The words were as much for me as they were for her. "Stephen and I have differences too. But we never argue. People never believe it when we say that, but it's true. Nothing is more important than our relationship with each other and with God. When we are asked to choose between our love for each other or being right when we have a disagreement, our love always wins. So we never start an argument. I would rather be right and say I am wrong and keep our love intact than to fight for the right to be right and lose our love."

That's probably the closest I have ever been to Rachel. I was playing the big sister role for the first time. I sure hope it was the right advice.

CHAPTER
16

Out of Darkness

Jonathan married Deborah the year after father died. She really was like mother. She could sing, she could paint, and she loved Jonathan like mother loved my father. Waiting on the right one to come along was the right choice for him.

Rachel and Samuel had another child. His name was Jacob. And Leah still talks about Popo. The old Rachel who was full of joy all the time was back! Children have a way of keeping us in the race. They trust us to do the right thing. And they should. It's a commandment. Or at least, it should be!

Stephen and I did not have children yet. We wanted to have a family and we tried, but we both knew the time had to be right. We believed that God would give us a family. But, somehow, in the back of my mind, there was a lingering doubt. I remembered dreaming about lost children and not finding them.

Maybe that was a sign that I was not meant to be a mother. If I was a mother, maybe I would lose my child and not ever find it again. I don't know. You just begin to think all kinds of things when your life doesn't seem to go the direction you think it should.

I couldn't remember the last time I had my recurring dream. When Jesus said he was the crashing wave and the children were like Donnie, the dreams went away. I thought that was all I needed to know since it didn't seem as important to me anymore. But I still thought about Jesus every day. It occurred to us that the day after we heard about father's death, while we were in Capernaum, we were going to hear the Rabbi talk to the people. We both had strong feelings about this Rabbi. We wouldn't say it aloud, but we both thought it. Stephen had even gone back to Capernaum and the surrounding area to see if he could find him. But no one knew where they had gone.

Then one day, Joda stopped by on his way to Jerusalem. He told us that he had heard that a good friend of the Rabbi who lived in Bethany was very ill.

"I heard this from Peter, who, by the way, has been following this Rabbi everywhere," said Joda. "He left his family and home to travel with this man. When they told the Rabbi about his friend, he did not go to see about him right away. He stayed away a day or two. Peter said that was not like him. But Stephen, they are all saying that this Rabbi can do miracles. He healed a blind man, a crippled man, he made a leper clean, and he even brought a little girl back to life! I am on my way to see this Rabbi."

"Who is this man?" asked Stephen. "We keep hearing about a mysterious Rabbi. Where is he from?"

"They say his name is Jesus and that he is from Nazareth. Isn't that were you were from before you married Sarina?"

Stephen looked at me and said nothing. We both knew that what we had suspected was true. But how could our friend, Jesus, do miracles? Even though we had seen it happen at Rachel's wedding, it just didn't seem possible. We didn't try to explain anything to Joda because we didn't know the answers ourselves for sure.

Stephen left with Joda for Bethany immediately. I wanted to go with him, but I had promised Rachel I would stay with her children while she went with Samuel to mourn the loss of one of his uncles.

When Stephen and Joda arrived, they learned that the Rabbi's friend was named Lazarus, and his sisters were Mary and Martha. But now Lazarus was dead, and he had been for four days. There were many mourners by the tomb and outside of the house where Mary and Martha lived. They did not understand why the Rabbi did not come right away. He loved their brother very much. Jesus and Lazarus had been friends for a long time.

Just as Stephen was about to ask someone about the details of Lazarus's death, he saw one of the sisters run past him. Someone was coming down the road, and there were many people surrounding him.

"My heart began to beat faster and faster as I felt something big was going to happen," he said as he told me all the details when he returned home.

"I tried to see past the crowd because I heard them repeating, 'Rabbi, Rabbi.' They were coming closer when I saw him for the first time. I know my heart stopped when I saw his face. It was him, Sarina! It was Jesus! He didn't see me at first. They went on to the tomb, and I hurried right behind them. Mary and Martha were both crying because he had not come sooner and now their brother was dead. Jesus just looked at them and I saw a tear in his eye."

Stephen was moved by this whole incident as I watched him tell the story, knowing that what he had seen was the proof he needed to believe all that Jesus had shared with him.

Stephen continued his story. "He walked toward the tomb and asked the men to roll the stone away. The men there objected, saying the smell would be overwhelming. He had been dead four days. But they did what he asked. The smell of death is awful, Sarina. But Jesus stood there and looked up to heaven. And then he cried out, 'Lazarus, come forth.' My heart was in my throat because I knew what he was asking for was impossible! This one act would either prove who he really was or it would be his death. In the next moment, there was a shadow coming from the tomb and then a light behind a figure of a man, a man who was wrapped in linen cloth, his burial clothes. It was Lazarus! He came out of the tomb and Jesus told them to unwrap him and give him food to eat. It was a miracle—Jesus brought him back to life! Everyone was gasping and crying and on their knees before Jesus. I saw it and I couldn't believe it!"

He was crying now as he told me this story. I felt chills run all over my body. He grabbed me and held me close to him. He was shaking.

"Stephen, did he see you there?" I asked.

"They took Lazarus to the house with his sisters. As Jesus turned to leave, He glanced my way and, yes, he saw me. Our eyes connected, but he did not come over. The crowd began to push against him, begging and pleading for healing of every kind. And he did heal many more that night until his men led him away for rest. We have to go back, Sarina, to talk to him. He told us that our friendship would be with him always. Surely he will talk to us."

"How can it be him, Stephen?" I said. "How can someone like you or me or our friend bring someone back to life? Is that possible?"

"Sarina, I don't know. I have to talk to him. I have so many questions to ask him. Years ago, when he told us who he thought he was, I was angry. I didn't believe it at first and then I thought his ideas would take him away from us, and they did. If it's all true, then he is the one who can free us from these Roman dogs who keep tormenting us. I just have to talk to him."

Somehow Stephen's ideas bothered me. There was anger in him when he talked about the Romans. And that was justified. But the depth of anger, the part of him that I didn't know, bothered me. And I kept asking myself how I felt about this truth we had discovered. Did I really believe it? I wanted to, but there was something keeping me from yielding to the idea that Jesus could be the Messiah.

We made our plans to go to Jerusalem on the next Passover which was not too far away. Jesus always made the trip for Passover when we were all together, so we knew he would be there. Stephen was excited, more excited than I had ever seen him. He seemed almost obsessed.

CHAPTER
17

Truth from the Garden

We arrived in Jerusalem the day Passover began. I had been there once before, but not when there were so many people. We were lucky to find a place to stay. We settled in and Stephen left to see if he could find any of Jesus's followers. I went to the market to buy the things we needed for the Passover Seder. I brought along my own utensils for preparation since you could never be sure what to find in Jerusalem. When I returned, I began cleaning the room. That's when Stephen came back.

"Sarina, come quickly. You have to see this," he said.

"What is it?" I asked. "Did you find him?"

He led me to the street near the temple, and I could see a crowd of people there, singing, dancing, and waving branches over their heads. It was a celebration! I had never seen this happening before.

"What's going on?" I asked Stephen.

"You'll see when he gets here," he said.

And then I saw it: a parade of people following behind a man on a donkey. As he came closer, I saw it was Jesus.

Everything this man, our good friend, did was so confusing. Why would he choose to ride a donkey into the city if he were truly the Messiah? Wouldn't he come in on a white horse with sword in hand? At least, that is Stephen's idea of the coming Messiah.

Everyone seemed to be celebrating! They were shouting praises to him! It was easy to get caught up in the excitement as we watched him pass. He had so many friends and followers. They just loved him!

Stephen smiled at my reaction to the crowd and what I had seen. He said he had something to tell me, so we returned to the room we had rented.

"We are meeting him in three days. One of his followers sent word. We are to meet him outside the eastern gate in the garden," Stephen exclaimed. He was so excited, he was almost out of breath.

"How did he know we were here?" I asked.

"That's what I asked the guy when he gave me the message. He said Jesus just knew we would be here and even where to find us. This man's name was Matthew, and he has been traveling with Jesus for the past three years. We talked for a while about all that has happened, and there is so much to tell, Sarina."

It was real. I wasn't dreaming. And now we were going to meet him. Stephen spent the whole night telling me what Matthew had shared with him.

"He told me of one time, Sarina, when they were near Capernaum. It had to be about the time of your father's death, and I believe if we had gone outside the city that next day, we would have witnessed it. There were thousands of people there on the hillside, and Jesus was teaching them. Matthew said he had been healing the sick and talking to the people for hours when they reminded him that the hour was late and the people were getting hungry. Matthew said Jesus told them to feed the crowd. He said they only had two fish and five loaves of bread. When Jesus saw this, he took it and blessed it and gave it back to the men and said, 'Give it to the people.' They did what he asked and they had enough to feed more than five thousand people and had baskets left over!"

Stephen continued to tell story after story up into the night. We were so happy we had come and that we were going to meet him soon. We only slept a couple of hours before dawn.

We were to meet him in the late afternoon on that third day. So for those days before, we looked around Jerusalem. Stephen went to the Temple and we had a great time together. This was special for us since we hadn't traveled here very often. We already had a great marriage and this was a blessing upon a blessing.

The time finally came for us to go to the garden outside the eastern gate. We had explicit directions on where to go, and the garden was beautiful. I had never been there before, but it reminded me of the feeling I would have down by the river at home. The peace was there. There were no crowds, there was a soft wind, and the fragrance in the air was familiar.

As we enjoyed the surroundings, we heard voices behind us. It was Jesus talking to his followers. We couldn't hear what he was telling them, but they left us. They didn't go far, but it was evident that Jesus wanted our time to be personal.

As he approached us, my heart jumped. I expected him to look different. But he looked just as he did several years ago down by the river. His smile was the same and his eyes were as blue now as they were then. He looked a little tired, but then he always did when we all went to the river. It was a time of rest.

"I'm so glad you came," he said. "It's been a long time."

CHAPTER 17

"Oh, Jesus, it's so good to see you," I said, hugging him tightly. Stephen and Jesus embraced, and we all sat under a tree overlooking the city.

"So much has happened. There is much to say and so little time." Jesus spoke with a touch of sadness in his voice.

"We have prayed for this day to come," said Stephen. "We now have the power to take what is ours and restore our nation!"

"Your words are true. But not in the way you think. Who am I, Stephen?" asked Jesus.

There was a long pause. As Stephen thought about what he wanted to say, Jesus looked at me. There was no longer the joyful smile I longed to see. Only a face with much wisdom and purpose. He turned back to Stephen.

Stephen said, "I saw you bring a man back to life, Jesus. You told us both who you were when we saw you at Rachel's wedding. You turned water into wine! I believe you are the Messiah. The one who has come to lead us against the Romans—to take back what is ours and was stolen—to battle mighty in the name of the God of Abraham!"

Jesus said, "It is true the God of Abraham has sent me to take back what was lost—but not the way you think. Not by the sword! Stephen, I come from a place of pure love where there is no pain, no tears, no fighting. God has anointed me to bring this good news to the poor, to proclaim freedom for the prisoners, and recovery of sight for the blind, to release the oppressed. But not by the sword! That is not His plan."

"Then what is His plan?" asked Stephen. "I don't understand."

I sat there with an uncontrollable fear coming over me. My stomach was beginning to hurt and a feeling of dread came over me. Jesus was silent for a moment before he tried to explain his true purpose for being here.

"I came to bring you hope. I came to teach what real love is—how loving God and each other can make the world right. I came to find the lost ones and to help them find their way back to their Creator. I came as the *ultimate sacrifice* for all the sin of the world. And this is God's plan—that I take on the sins of the world. I will be lifted up for all the world to see, and they will still not understand. It is as the mustard seed. It starts out as a small seed buried in the ground. But it grows to be the strongest tree of them all."

What was he saying? I heard his words and took them straight into my heart, but I still did not know what he was saying.

"You talk in riddles, Jesus," I said. "What are you telling us?"

"I will only be here a short while longer. Then you will not see me again. I will go to my Father and make a place for you to come later. I will be back for you. You must believe I can do this."

"Are you going to die?" I asked him.

"I'm going to live, Sarina. I'm going to live."

Stephen stood up without saying a word and started to leave. But Jesus stopped him.

"Don't be angry, Stephen," Jesus said. "You will understand when the time comes. I wanted this time with you both to tell you how much I love you. My time here with you was well spent. We learned a lot from each other, how to trust each other. Please, trust me now. And believe what I have said."

With those last words, he embraced me and touched Stephen's shoulder, and then he left us. Somehow I knew it would be the last time we would ever speak to him.

Stephen didn't say a word as we walked back into the city. When we got back to our room, he sat down and just stared at the walls. Then he told me he would be back soon. And he left.

I tried to go over all the things that had happened but everything was so mixed up. Things were confusing. I wasn't even sure I remembered everything Jesus had said to us. But the one thing that kept going over and over in my mind were the words *ultimate sacrifice*. I thought about my dream and how Jesus said he was the big wave and would save the children. I tried to tie it together, but it wasn't clear. What was I missing? It had been several hours when I heard Stephen return.

"Sarina, are you awake?" he asked.

"Yes, I am," I said. "Is everything okay?"

"I'm not sure," said Stephen. "I've been talking to different ones about Jesus and he has a lot of enemies. I thought they all liked him. They were singing to him and praising him three days ago. But the priests are not happy with him. They don't believe him. And they want to arrest him."

"Arrest him?" I asked. "For what? What has he done to make them want him in prison?"

"Sarina, they don't believe he is the Son of God. They are calling him a blasphemer. I just pray his followers are taking him away from here. Things need to settle down before he comes back."

"But he won't leave before Passover, will he? He is always here for Passover. What will they do to him if they arrest him?" I asked.

"They won't arrest him. They'll have to find him first," said Stephen.

I remember lying there most of the night, thinking about all the "what ifs." What if they find him and arrest him? What if they want to punish him? What if they never find him and we never see him again? What if . . . it was too much. I closed my eyes, and still sleep did not come. Stephen tossed and turned all night. When the sun came into the room at dawn, we were both lying there with our eyes wide open.

CHAPTER

18

Reassurance

That day we decided to go to Bethany. We wanted to meet this man called Lazarus. Stephen showed me the tomb where Lazarus had been buried, and then we went up to the house. Two men were leaving as we approached.

"How can I help you?" asked one of the sisters.

"My name is Stephen, and this is my wife, Sarina. We are good friends of Jesus."

"Come in, please," said Mary. She smiled and treated us as though we were family.

"Brother, this is Stephen, and this is his wife, Sarina," said Mary. "And this is my sister, Martha. They are good friends of Jesus."

I stared at Lazarus as though I expected him to be ill. He was as healthy as anyone else I saw that day.

"My husband was here when Jesus . . ." I began to weep. "When Jesus brought you back from the dead!"

Lazarus took my hand and we all went out to the garden. We sat there for hours, listening to him tell us about his friendship with Jesus. He used to come and work for Lazarus when he was younger. Stephen never came on these trips because it was so far away from Nazareth. Jesus would come with Joseph when they were traveling to Jerusalem together. Mary and Martha were about the same age as Jesus, and they had a great friendship as well. There was nothing out of the ordinary until the last two or three years when Jesus started his following.

When I asked him what he remembered about the miracle, he didn't remember much. But he knew he was dead and now he was alive. He said he remembers darkness all around him, and then he saw a tiny spot of light. And it was like it exploded and he was alive! No pain! He could breathe!

I found a reassurance in what he was saying. Resurrection was a miracle by God used for His glory and for nothing else. It was a definite possibility. This man had experienced it.

Stephen and I left Bethany and arrived back in Jerusalem right after dark. We prepared the Passover and decided we would leave for home in the morning. We did sleep better that night than we did the night before.

CHAPTER
19

The Silent Darkness

We woke to a light rain and a little thunder in the distance. It was cool and breezy. After a while, I began to assemble things for the trip home when Stephen decided to go to the market for supplies. He wasn't gone ten minutes when he stormed back in the room.

"They arrested him! Last night! They arrested him!" he cried.

"What?" I asked. "Where is he now?"

"They had him at the governor's palace! He left it up to the people. Half of them cried 'save him' and the other half cried 'kill him!' It's crazy! The whole world is crazy!"

"Let's go," I said. "We have to see what happens!"

"No, Sarina. You stay here. I don't want you there. Stay here where you will be safe!" Stephen said.

"I'm going, Stephen. He's my friend, too, and I won't desert him at a time like this!"

"It's too late. They already condemned him. They are mocking him and spitting on him. It's awful, Sarina. You don't need to see it. They are going to crucify him."

"What has he done? He didn't hurt anyone! They can't do that! Can they?"

I started crying uncontrollably, and Stephen took me in his arms. He was crying, too, but he didn't want me to see. What a horrible way to die! Where were his followers? Why didn't they protect him?

"We have to go see, Stephen," I said. "We have to go be there."

Through the light rain, we approached the western gate where they had taken him. It was so crowded. People were everywhere, pushing and shoving. Some were running the other direction, away from the gate, while others were huddled together crying. Others seemed pleased with the situation and were going about their daily tasks, some joking and laughing, some even unaware of what was going on.

When we came out of the gate, we could see the hill and there were three crosses standing upright. We ran up the hill to get closer so we could see and the soldiers started pushing us back. When we were as close as we could be, we could see he was already on the cross they had made, with his hands nailed and tied, along with his feet nailed to the bottom. They had made a crown out of thorny vines, and they must have forced it on his head because there was blood trickling down his face. I began to feel sick. It hurt me to see him like this. He didn't deserve this treatment. Jesus was a gentle man and never hurt anyone. Why would they treat him this way?

I saw Mary there with one of his followers. I think it was John. But the other men were not around, just the soldiers, yelling out, mocking him. They were calling him names.

The weather began to get worse, with thunder and lightning hitting all over. It started raining harder and many people were scrambling to leave. But the soldiers still would not let us approach.

I don't think Jesus saw us. I couldn't look at him because he had been severely beaten and he was bleeding so badly, I was physically hurting inside. I was literally sick to my stomach. If he was the Son of God, why would God let him suffer like this? He didn't do anything wrong! I was not understanding this. It's too much. This is just too much for me to handle.

He said something to his mother, but I couldn't hear his words. It was raining so hard, you couldn't hear anything. Stephen was just holding me tighter and tighter as I buried my head into his chest. Then Jesus spoke again. All I could make out was, "Forgive them Father," and a few moments later, Stephen told me he took his last breath.

I began to cry and sob until the rain suddenly stopped. There was dead silence. Then the earth began to shake and the thunder and lightning boomed overhead and people began to run. The soldiers ushered us away with their swords toward the gate. They let Mary, John, and a couple of others with her stay to take the body away.

We stood there in the rain, frozen in disbelief as we watched them take him down off the cross and his mother hold his head in her hands.

We heard later that they had taken his body away for burial nearby. We didn't see any of the other followers around anywhere. They just abandoned him. How could they do that? They saw the miracles. They were there when the miracles happened! What were they afraid of?

Stephen and I just stood there in the rain until the soldiers moved us along. We walked away in a daze, not saying a word to each other, just holding on tightly.

Inside, I felt like everything I ever knew and trusted about God was wrong. If Jesus was the Son of God, why would God let Him die like this? If I had a child that I loved passionately, I would never let harm come to him, not like this. Not the physical pain he suffered, the humiliation without justification. He was innocent! The God I knew would not do that! The God I thought I knew would have compassion. Where is the justice? Where is the unconditional, uncompromising Love?

What if what Jesus said and believed was wrong? He was our friend, a normal person like Stephen and me. What if what he said about preparing a place for us doesn't happen? What is death anyway? Seems like I should know this answer by now.

I tried to recall the words that Jesus said in the garden earlier in the week. I remember he said to trust him. It was easy to trust him when he was alive. How am I supposed to trust him now?

I felt so empty inside. I was exhausted, and Stephen wasn't talking about it at all. He had retreated inside himself. I never saw him like this. We reached out to each other, but we just couldn't talk about it. This whole part of our life had gone much deeper than we ever thought anything could. How will we ever come out of this?

Do Dreams Come True?

We had been home for a few days away from that city with the cruel people and the righteous priests who were afraid of their own shadows. Stephen was quiet. He would smile at me and tell me he loves me, but he didn't talk about Jesus. We never found Mary that night. We did look for her, but everyone just vanished.

I needed to see my family. So we stopped by our house first to take care of a few things. I thought about going down to the river, but I wanted to visit the family first. It had been quite a while since we had been down there. In fact, it was when Jesus was still going there with us.

The house Stephen built for us was right outside of Nazareth, about half a day's walk to Cana. We stopped by Rachel and Samuel's house, but they were not there. They must have taken a trip. I had heard earlier that Samuel wanted to move the family to Jericho because there was a job opportunity there that would benefit the family. Rachel didn't want to leave the area because it was so far away from family. Maybe they went to see what he had in mind.

So we went on to Capernaum to see Aunt Shalee and Joda. I hadn't seen Donnie and the other kids in a long time, and I really missed them.

When we got there, everyone was scattered all over. Joda was out fishing and the kids were here and there. I asked my aunt where Donnie was.

"He's down by the sea," said Aunt Shalee who was looking happier than I had ever seen her. "Why don't you go down and find him?"

"I think I will," I said. And I started out while Stephen stayed and talked with my aunt.

When I got down to the water, I couldn't find Mira. She was always with Donnie and they were nowhere to be found. I walked over to the grove of trees by the bank of the north side of the sea, and I asked the men there if they knew where to find Donnie or Mira.

"He's here. We just saw him a few minutes ago. Try there, behind those boats. I think he just came back in."

What did he mean "just came back in"? I walked over to the boats, and as I looked around, I saw him sitting in a chair close to the sea.

"Are you looking for me?" said the voice behind her.

"Joda!" I said. "How are you?"

"Great! I bet you are looking for Donnie. He's right over there," he said. "I think he's been wanting to see you!"

I turned and ran to the chair and there he was. Big smile on his face! Excitement in his eyes! There was something different about him that day. He seemed more connected than usual.

"Hello Donnie," I said as I gave him a big hug. "I have missed you so much."

SARINA

He took his hands and put them on each side of my face, drew me in, and looked at me straight in my eyes.

"I have missed you, too, Aunt Sarina," he said softly.

In that moment, time stopped. Is this another dream? I have not ever heard this voice before. Yet it is so familiar. There is a stirring in my spirit, a joy I can't explain. A well of emotions began to pour out and tears started to flow for both of us. We hugged each other so tightly. Donnie was back from wherever he had been the last thirty years. He is here, right now!

"How—when did—what happened?" I asked.

"It was Jesus," said Donnie. "At the wedding when Rachel got married, he said that one day I would be whole again, like I was before in Ramah. I understood him and I believed—I have always heard what people say. And I will always remember how wonderful you were to me, how much you loved me!"

"But I've seen you since the wedding," I said. "When did this happen?"

"It was during Passover, just a few days ago. I saw Jesus in one of my dreams. He came in like a crashing wave and found me on the shore of the beach. He appeared to me in a dazzling white robe, and he wrapped his arms around me, and I felt all warm inside. It was just like your dream, Sarina. Just like the one you shared with me before. When I woke up, I felt stronger than I ever have before. I was more alert. When Mira came in to help me get ready for the day, I just said, 'I can dress myself today.' And she fainted. So I helped *her* get ready for the day."

We both laughed. Maybe a little too much. But for me, it was to help cover the myriad of emotions I was feeling in my heart. He was so full of life now, and this was a personal miracle for me as well as Donnie. This made me miss my dear friend all the more now.

"I have always loved you, Donnie. Your eyes showed me your heart. I am so happy for you. This miracle has made my memories of Jesus more precious than ever."

"He's not dead, Sarina," he said. "You have to trust me. He said you would have a hard time believing it."

"That is hard to believe, Donnie. I-I saw Him die!"

"I've seen Him," said Donnie. "He came by the shore a couple of days ago to see me. He said I was blessed because I believe in Him."

"Donnie, I'm so happy for you," I said. "I prayed for this so many times over the years and now this miracle has happened. Thank you, Jehovah God."

God and I were not on especially good terms right now, but I still felt inclined to thank Him for this miracle. Donnie deserved this. It was justified and he was innocent when it happened to him. That is mercy!

"Let's go up to the house and talk to Stephen," I said. "He will be so surprised to see you. He needs a miracle like this one right now."

We returned to Aunt Shalee's house and spent the rest of the day rejoicing in the miracle that Donnie was made whole. I've never seen my aunt happier.

The impact of this latest miracle was most evident upon Stephen. When he first heard Donnie speak, he fell to the ground on his knees and just wept almost uncontrollably. I watched him release all those doubts he had about Jesus, and from that moment on, he never questioned any of the choices Jesus had made. Even though he was now able to deal with Jesus's death, he knew that I still had some issues that I would have to work through on my own.

CHAPTER

Back to the River

We left for home the next day. Even though there was much to rejoice about, we still thought about Jesus every day. I began to remember how it felt when my mother died. That hadn't happened in many years now. I couldn't seem to put it all behind me: the ups and downs of knowing Jesus, his death "so we could live" stories, his cruel punishment . . . how could God allow his son to go through all that?

"Ultimate sacrifice," "I came to bring hope," "I came for all," "Trust me," "He's here, find Him," "I'm going to live!" All those words just seemed to keep popping up in my head. Why was it so hard to just believe that what He said was the truth? He was my friend and I trusted Him with my life. He knew all my secrets and He even knew my heart. He would never lie to me. I was tired of holding all this in.

I decided to make a trip to the river where we all met many years ago. It was a day much like that first day, with a warm breeze singing through the trees. The old tree hung out over the river bigger than ever. I could almost hear our voices as I thought back over all the conversations we had there—mother's voice, Stephen's voice, Jesus' voice. I could even imagine the fragrance that lingered every time Jesus was around.

Why was it so hard for me to let go of things I find hard to believe? I didn't see Jesus bring Lazarus out of that tomb! I didn't see Jesus after He died! I wasn't there when Donnie was healed! But I did dream the dream that was used to heal Donnie. God used me, a nobody, so He must be using Jesus as the crashing wave to save us all.

It was time to just believe it. All the things that happened in my life were for a reason. The fight was over now, and I would just have to believe all the things Jesus told me.

It was like a gradual release of tension in my head. I felt a physical calm come over my body as I sat there, looking out over the river. I could hear the birds singing and it felt just like it did the day we all met years ago. Oh, how I wish we could go back in time.

And then a sudden peace came over me. It came when I let everything go. It was the calm I felt after the wave crashed over me in my dream, after I felt the wave's edge on my face, I was safe, and I knew that everything that had happened was real and true. I discovered that I was the child I was looking for, and I knew that Jesus had come to save *me*.

And then I felt a hand on my shoulder. As I turned around, the reflection from the brilliant white robe made my eyes water. And the fragrance became stronger as I looked into His eyes, His deep, blue eyes.

The End

About the Author

Beverly Forgus is a freelance writer, playwright, poet, and songwriter. Much of her writing is Christian inspired as she grew up in the church, and she and her husband are currently involved in leading the Prayer Ministry at Citymark Church in League City, Texas.

While traveling in Israel, she was inspired by the towns in Galilee, particularly Nazareth, Cana, and Nain. Wondering what it would be like to live there two thousand years ago, she began to create stories in her mind about characters we already know about from the Bible. And Sarina was born.

She has written Christian gospel songs that were recorded and produced in North Carolina. Copies of the album, *Aldersgate Praise*, were sold when she performed with a gospel group in various venues across the country.

Her joy for writing has been with her since she was a child. She would make up fantasies and perform plays in the living room of her home. She wants to pass this imagination and love for the arts on to her readers!

She is a Texan and lives in La Marque, Texas, with her husband, Steve. Now that she is retired, she can spend all her time writing. And she loves it! You can email her at bevforgus@comcast.net.

CPSIA information can be obtained
at www.ICGtesting.com
Printed in the USA
FSHW01n0648100718
50335FS